MW00509128

Father Sergius

Father Sergius

LEO TOLSTOY

Translated by
Louise and Aylmer Maude

WILDSIDE PRESS
Doylestown, Pennsylvania

Father Sergius
A publication of
Wildside Press
P.O. Box 301
Holicong, PA 18928-0301

www.wildsidepress.com

Chapter I

*I*n Petersburg in the eighteen-forties a surprising event occurred. An officer of the Cuirassier Life Guards, a handsome prince who everyone predicted would become aide-de-camp to the Emperor Nicholas I and have a brilliant career, left the service, broke off his engagement to a beautiful maid of honor, a favorite of the Empress's, gave his small estate to his sister, and retired to a monastery to become a monk.

This event appeared extraordinary and inexplicable to those who did not know his inner motives, but for Prince Stepan Kasatsky himself it all occurred so naturally that he could not imagine how he could have acted otherwise.

His father, a retired colonel of the Guards, had died when Stepan was twelve, and sorry as his mother was to part from her son, she entered him at the Military College as her deceased husband had intended.

The widow herself, with her daughter, Varvara, moved to Petersburg to be near her son and have him with her for the holidays.

The boy was distinguished both by his brilliant ability and by his immense self-esteem. He was first both in his studies — especially in mathematics, of which he was particularly fond — and also in drill and in riding. Though of more than average height, he was handsome and agile, and he would have been an altogether exemplary cadet had it not been for his quick temper. He was remarkably truthful, and was neither dissipated nor addicted to drink. The only faults that marred his conduct were fits of fury to which he was subject and during which he lost control of himself and became like a wild animal. He once nearly threw out of the window another cadet who had begun to tease him about his collection of minerals. On another occasion he came almost completely to grief by flinging a whole dish of cutlets at an officer who was acting as steward, attacking him and, it was said, striking him for having broken his word and told a barefaced lie. He would certainly have been reduced to the ranks had not the Director of the College hushed up the whole matter and dismissed the steward.

By the time he was eighteen he had finished his College course and received a commission as lieutenant in an aristocratic regiment of the Guards.

The Emperor Nicholas Pavlovich (Nicholas I) had noticed him while he was still at the College, and continued to take notice of him in the regiment, and it was on this account that people predicted for him an appointment as aide-de-camp to the Emperor. Kasatsky himself strongly desired it, not from ambition only but chiefly because since his cadet days he had been passionately devoted to Nicholas

Pavlovich. The Emperor had often visited the Military College and every time Kasatsky saw that tall erect figure, with breast expanded in its military overcoat, entering with brisk step, saw the cropped side-whiskers, the moustache, the aquiline nose, and heard the sonorous voice exchanging greetings with the cadets, he was seized by the same rapture that he experienced later on when he met the woman he loved. Indeed, his passionate adoration of the Emperor was even stronger: he wished to sacrifice something — everything, even himself — to prove his complete devotion. And the Emperor Nicholas was conscious of evoking this rapture and deliberately aroused it. He played with the cadets, surrounded himself with them, treating them sometimes with childish simplicity, sometimes as a friend, and then again with majestic solemnity. After that affair with the officer, Nicholas Pavlovich said nothing to Kasatsky, but when the latter approached he waved him away theatrically, frowned, shook his finger at him, and afterwards when leaving, said: "Remember that I know everything. There are some things I would rather not know, but they remain here," and he pointed to his heart.

When on leaving College the cadets were received by the Emperor, he did not again refer to Kasatsky's offence, but told them all, as was his custom, that they should serve him and the fatherland loyally, that he would always be their best friend, and that when necessary they might approach him direct. All the cadets were as usual greatly moved, and Kasatsky even shed tears, remembering the past, and vowed that he would serve his beloved Tsar with all his soul.

When Kasatsky took up his commission his mother moved with her daughter first to Moscow and then to their country estate. Kasatsky gave half his property to his sister and kept only enough to maintain himself in the expensive regiment he had joined.

To all appearance he was just an ordinary, brilliant young officer of the Guards making a career for himself; but intense and complex strivings went on within him. From early childhood his efforts had seemed to be very varied, but essentially they were all one and the same. He tried in everything he took up to attain such success and perfection as would evoke praise and surprise. Whether it was his studies or his military exercises, he took them up and worked at them till he was praised and held up as an example to others. Mastering one subject he took up another, and obtained first place in his studies. For example, while still at College he noticed in himself an awkwardness in French conversation, and contrived to master French till he spoke it as well as Russian, and then he took up chess and became an excellent player.

Apart from his main vocation, which was the service of his Tsar and the fatherland, he always set himself some particular aim, and however unimportant it was, devoted himself completely to it and lived for it until it was accomplished. And as soon as it was attained another aim would immediately present itself, replacing its predecessor. This passion for distinguishing himself, or for accomplishing something in order to distinguish himself, filled his life. On taking up his commission he set himself to acquire the utmost perfection in knowledge of the service, and very soon became a model officer, though still with the same fault of ungovernable irascibility, which here in the service again led him to commit actions inimical to his success. Then he took to reading, having once in conversation in society felt himself deficient in general education — and again achieved his purpose. Then, wishing to secure a brilliant position in high society, he learnt to dance excellently and very soon was invited to all the balls in the best circles, and to some of their evening gatherings. But this did not satisfy him: he was accustomed to being first, and in this society was far from being so.

The highest society then consisted, and I think always consist, of four sorts of people: rich people who are received at Court, people not wealthy but born and brought up in Court circles, rich people who ingratiate themselves into the Court set, and people neither rich nor belonging to the Court but who ingratiate themselves into the first and second sets.

Kasatsky did not belong to the first two sets, but was readily welcomed in the others. On entering society he determined to have relations with some society lady, and to his own surprise quickly accomplished this purpose. He soon realized, however, that the circles in which he moved were not the highest, and that though he was received in the highest spheres he did not belong to them. They were polite to him, but showed by their whole manner that they had their own set and that he was not of it. And Kasatsky wished to belong to that inner circle. To attain that end it would be necessary to be an aide-de-camp to the Emperor — which he expected to become — or to marry into that exclusive set, which he resolved to do. And his choice fell on a beauty belonging to the Court, who not merely belonged to the circle into which he wished to be accepted, but whose friendship was coveted by the very highest people and those most firmly established in that highest circle. This was Countess Korotkova. Kasatsky began to pay court to her, and not merely for the sake of his career. She was extremely attractive and he soon fell in love with her. At first she was noticeably cool towards him, but then suddenly changed and became gracious, and her mother gave him pressing invitations to visit them. Kasatsky proposed and was accepted. He was surprised at the facility with which he attained such happiness. But though he noticed something strange and unusual in the behavior towards him of both mother and daughter, he was blinded by being so deeply in love, and did not realize what almost the whole town knew — namely, that his fiancée had been the Emperor Nicholas's mistress the previous year.

Two weeks before the day arranged for the wedding, Kasatsky was at Tsarskoe Selo at his fiancée's country place. It was a hot day in May. He and his betrothed had walked about the garden and were sitting on a bench in a shady linden alley. Mary's white muslin dress suited

her particularly well, and she seemed the per-
sonification of innocence and love as she sat,
now bending her head, now gazing up at the
very tall and handsome man who was speaking
to her with particular tenderness and self-re-
straint, as if he feared by word or gesture to
offend or sully her angelic purity.

Kasatsky belonged to those men of the
eighteen-forties (they are now no longer to be
found) who while deliberately and without any
conscientious scruples condoning impurity in
themselves, required ideal and angelic purity in
their women, regarded all unmarried women of
their circle as possessed of such purity, and
treated them accordingly. There was much that
was false and harmful in this outlook, as con-
cerning the laxity the men permitted themselves, but in regard to the women that old-fash-
ioned view (sharply differing from that held by
young people today who see in every girl merely
a female seeking a mate) was, I think, of value.
The girls, perceiving such adoration, endeav-
ored with more or less success to be goddesses.

Such was the view Kasatsky held of women, and that was how he regarded his fiancée. He was particularly in love that day, but did not experience any sensual desire for her. On the contrary he regarded her with tender adoration as something unattainable.

He rose to his full height, standing before her with both hands on his saber.

"I have only now realized what happiness a man can experience! And it is you, my darling, who have given me this happiness," he said with a timid smile.

Endearments had not yet become usual between them, and feeling himself morally inferior he felt terrified at this stage to use them to such an angel.

"It is thanks to you that I have come to know myself. I have learnt that I am better than I thought."

"I have known that for a long time. That was why I began to love you."

Nightingales trilled near by and the fresh leafage rustled, moved by a passing breeze.

He took her hand and kissed it, and tears came into his eyes.

She understood that he was thanking her for having said she loved him. He silently took a few steps up and down, and then approached her again and sat down.

"You know . . . I have to tell you . . . I was not disinterested when I began to make love to you. I wanted to get into society; but later . . . how unimportant that became in comparison with you — when I got to know you. You are not angry with me for that?"

She did not reply but merely touched his hand. He understood that this meant: "No, I am not angry."

"You said . . ." He hesitated. It seemed too bold to say. "You said that you began to love me. I believe it — but there is something that troubles you and checks your feeling. What is it?"

"Yes — now or never!" thought she. "He is bound to know of it anyway. But now he will not forsake me. Ah, if he should, it would be terrible!" And she threw a loving glance at his tall, noble, powerful figure. She loved him now more than she had loved the Tsar, and apart from the Imperial dignity would not have preferred the Emperor to him.

"Listen! I cannot deceive you. I have to tell you. You ask what it is? It is that I have loved before."

She again laid her hand on his with an imploring gesture. He was silent.

"You want to know who it was? It was — the Emperor."

"We all love him. I can imagine you, a schoolgirl at the Institute . . ."

"No, it was later. I was infatuated, but it passed . . . I must tell you . . ."

"Well, what of it?"

"No, it was not simply —" She covered her face with her hands.

"What? You gave yourself to him?"

She was silent.

"His mistress?"

She did not answer.

He sprang up and stood before her with trembling jaws, pale as death. He now remembered how the Emperor, meeting him on the Nevsky, had amiably congratulated him.

"O God, what have I done! Stiva!"

"Don't touch me! Don't touch me! Oh, how it pains!"

He turned away and went to the house. There he met her mother.

"What is the matter, Prince? I . . ." She became silent on seeing his face. The blood had suddenly rushed to his head.

"You knew it, and used me to shield them! If you weren't a woman. . . !" he cried, lifting his enormous fist, and turning aside he ran away.

Had his fiancée's lover been a private person he would have killed him, but it was his beloved Tsar.

Next day he applied both for furlough and his discharge, and professing to be ill, so as to see no one, he went away to the country.

He spent the summer at his village arranging his affairs. When summer was over he did not return to Petersburg, but entered a monastery and there became a monk.

His mother wrote to try to dissuade him from this decisive step, but he replied that he felt God's call which transcended all other considerations. Only his sister, who was as proud and ambitious as he, understood him.

She understood that he had become a monk in order to be above those who considered themselves his superiors. And she understood him correctly. By becoming a monk he showed contempt for all that seemed most important to others and had seemed so to him while he was in the service, and he now ascended a height from which he could look down on those he had formerly envied. . . . But it was not this alone, as his sister Varvara supposed, that influenced him. There was also in him something else — a sincere religious feeling which Varvara did not know, which intertwined itself with the feeling of pride and the desire for pre-eminence, and guided him. His disillusionment with Mary, whom he had thought of angelic purity, and his sense of injury, were so strong that they brought him to despair, and the despair led him — to what? To God, to his childhood's faith which had never been destroyed in him.

Chapter II

*K*asatsky entered the monastery on the feast of the Intercession of the Blessed Virgin. The Abbot of that monastery was a gentleman by birth, a learned writer and a starets, that is, he belonged to that succession of monks originating in Walachia who each choose a director and teacher whom they implicitly obey. This Superior had been a disciple of the starets Ambrose, who was a disciple of Makarius, who was a disciple of the starets Leonid, who was a disciple of Paussy Velichkovsky.

To this Abbot Kasatsky submitted himself as to his chosen director. Here in the monastery, besides the feeling of ascendancy over others that such a life gave him, he felt much as he had done in the world: he found satisfaction in attaining the greatest possible perfection outwardly as well as inwardly. As in the regiment he had been not merely an irreproachable officer but had even exceeded his duties and widened the borders of perfection, so also as a monk he tried to be perfect, and was always industrious, abstemious, submissive, and meek, as well as pure both in deed and in thought, and obedient. This last quality in particular made life far easier for him. If many of the demands of life in the monastery, which was near the capital and much frequented, did not please him and were temptations to him, they were all nullified by obedience: "It is not for me to reason; my business is to do the task set me, whether it be standing beside the relics, singing in the choir, or making up accounts in the monastery guest-house." All possibility of doubt about anything was silenced by obedience to the starets. Had it not been for this, he would have been oppressed by the length and monotony of the church services, the bustle of the many visitors, and the bad qualities of the other monks. As it was, he not only bore it all joyfully but found in it solace and support. "I don't know why it is necessary to hear the same prayers several times a day, but I know that it is necessary; and knowing this I find joy in them." His director told him that as material food is necessary for the maintenance of the life of the body, so spiritual food — the church prayers — is necessary for the maintenance of the spiritual life. He believed this, and though the church services, for which he had to get up early in the morning, were a difficulty, they certainly calmed him and gave him joy. This was the result of his consciousness of humility, and the certainty that whatever he had to do, being fixed by the starets, was right.

The interest of his life consisted not only in an ever greater and greater subjugation of his will, but in the attainment of all the Christian virtues, which at first seemed to him easily attainable. He had given his whole estate to his sister and did not regret it, he had no personal claims, humility towards his inferiors was not merely easy for him but afforded him pleasure. Even victory over the sins of the flesh, greed and lust, was easily attained. His director had specially warned him against the latter sin, but Kasatsky felt free from it and was glad.

One thing only tormented him — the remembrance of his fiancée; and not merely the remembrance but the vivid image of what might have been. Involuntarily he recalled a lady he knew who had been a favorite of the Emperor's, but had afterwards married and become an admirable wife and mother. The husband had a high position, influence and honor, and a good and penitent wife.

In his better hours Kasatsky was not disturbed by such thoughts, and when he recalled them at such times he was merely glad to feel that the temptation was past. But there were moments when all that made up his present life suddenly grew dim before him, moments when, if he did not cease to believe in the aims he had set himself, he ceased to see them and could evoke no confidence in them but was seized by a remembrance of, and — terrible to say — a regret for, the change of life he had made.

The only thing that saved him in that state of mind was obedience and work, and the fact that the whole day was occupied by prayer. He went through the usual forms of prayer, he bowed in prayer, he even prayed more than usual, but it was lip-service only and his soul was not in it. This condition would continue for a day, or sometimes for two days, and would then pass of itself. But those days were dreadful. Kasatsky felt that he was neither in his own hands nor in God's, but was subject to some-thing else. All he could do then was to obey the starets, to restrain himself, to undertake noth-ing, and simply to wait. In general all this time he lived not by his own will but by that of the starets, and in this obedience he found a special tranquility.

So he lived in his first monastery for seven

years. At the end of the third year he received
the tonsure and was ordained to the priesthood
by the name of Sergius. The profession was an
important event in his inner life. He had previously experienced a great consolation and
spiritual exaltation when receiving communion,
and now when he himself officiated, the per-
formance of the preparation filled him with
ecstatic and deep emotion. But subsequently
that feeling became more and more deadened,
and once when he was officiating in a depressed
state of mind he felt that the influence pro-
duced on him by the service would not endure.
And it did in fact weaken till only the habit
remained.

In general in the seventh year of his life
in the monastery Sergius grew weary. He had
learnt all there was to learn and had attained all
there was to attain, there was nothing more to
do and his spiritual drowsiness increased. During this time he heard of his mother's death and
his sister Varvara's marriage, but both events
were matters of indifference to him. His whole

attention and his whole interest were concentrated on his inner life.

In the fourth year of his priesthood, during which the Bishop had been particularly kind to him, the starets told him that he ought not to decline it if he were offered an appointment to higher duties. Then monastic ambition, the very thing he had found so repulsive in other monks, arose within him. He was assigned to a monastery near the metropolis. He wished to refuse but the starets ordered him to accept the appointment. He did so, and took leave of the starets and moved to the other monastery.

The exchange into the metropolitan monastery was an important event in Sergius's life. There he encountered many temptations, and his whole will-power was concentrated on meeting them.

In the first monastery, women had not been a temptation to him, but here that temptation arose with terrible strength and even took definite shape. There was a lady known for her frivolous behavior who began to seek his favor.

She talked to him and asked him to visit her. Sergius sternly declined, but was horrified by the definiteness of his desire. He was so alarmed that he wrote about it to the starets. And in addition, to keep himself in hand, he spoke to a young novice and, conquering his sense of shame, confessed his weakness to him, asking him to keep watch on him and not let him go anywhere except to service and to fulfill his duties.

Besides this, a great pitfall for Sergius lay in the fact of his extreme antipathy to his new Abbot, a cunning worldly man who was making a career for himself in the Church. Struggle with himself as he might, he could not master that feeling. He was submissive to the Abbot, but in the depths of his soul he never ceased to condemn him. And in the second year of his residence at the new monastery that ill-feeling broke out.

The Vigil service was being performed in the large church on the eve of the feast of the Intercession of the Blessed Virgin, and there were many visitors. The Abbot himself was conducting the service. Father Sergius was standing in his usual place and praying: that is, he was in that condition of struggle which always occupied him during the service, especially in the large church when he was not himself conducting the service. This conflict was occasioned by his irritation at the presence of fine folk, especially ladies. He tried not to see them or to notice all that went on: how a soldier conducted them, pushing the common people aside, how the ladies pointed out the monks to one another — especially himself and a monk noted for his good looks. He tried as it were to keep his mind in blinkers, to see nothing but the light of the candles on the altar-screen, the icons, and those conducting the service. He tried to hear nothing but the prayers that were being chanted or read, to feel nothing but self-oblivion in consciousness of the fulfillment of duty — a feeling he always experienced when hearing or reciting in advance the prayers he had so often heard.

So he stood, crossing and prostrating

himself when necessary, and struggled with himself, now giving way to cold condemnation and now to a consciously evoked obliteration of thought and feeling. Then the sacristan, Father Nicodemus — also a great stumbling-block to Sergius who involuntarily reproached him for flattering and fawning on the Abbot — approached him and, bowing low, requested his presence behind the holy gates. Father Sergius straightened his mantle, put on his biretta, and went circumspectly through the crowd.

"*Lise, regarde a droite, c'est lui!*" he heard a woman's voice say.

"*Ou, ou? Il n'est pas tellement beau.*"

He knew that they were speaking of him. He heard them and, as always at moments of temptation, he repeated the words, "Lead us not into temptation," and bowing his head and lowering his eyes went past the ambo and in by the north door, avoiding the canons in their cassocks who were just then passing the altar-screen. On entering the sanctuary he bowed, crossing himself as usual and bending double before the icons. Then, raising his head but without turning, he glanced out of the corner of his eye at the Abbot, whom he saw standing beside another glittering figure.

The Abbot was standing by the wall in his vestments. Having freed his short plump hands from beneath his chasuble he had folded them over his fat body and protruding stomach, and fingering the cords of his vestments was smilingly saying something to a military man in the uniform of a general of the Imperial suite, with its insignia and shoulder-knots which Father Sergius's experienced eye at once recognized. This general had been the commander of the regiment in which Sergius had served. He now evidently occupied an important position, and Father Sergius at once noticed that the Abbot was aware of this and that his red face and bald head beamed with satisfaction and pleasure. This vexed and disgusted Father Sergius, the more so when he heard that the Abbot had only sent for him to satisfy the general's curiosity to see a man who had formerly served with him, as he expressed it.

"Very pleased to see you in your angelic guise," said the general, holding out his hand. "I hope you have not forgotten an old comrade."

The whole thing — the Abbot's red, smiling face amid its fringe of grey, the general's words, his well-cared-for face with its self-satisfied smile and the smell of wine from his breath and of cigars from his whiskers — revolted Father Sergius. He bowed again to the Abbot and said:

"Your reverence deigned to send for me?" — and stopped, the whole expression of his face and eyes asking why.

"Yes, to meet the General," replied the Abbot.

"Your reverence, I left the world to save myself from temptation," said Father Sergius, turning pale and with quivering lips. "Why do you expose me to it during prayers and in God's house?"

"You may go! Go!" said the Abbot, flaring up and frowning.

Next day Father Sergius asked pardon of the Abbot and of the brethren for his pride, but at the same time, after a night spent in prayer, he decided that he must leave this monastery, and he wrote to the starets begging permission to return to him. He wrote that he felt his weakness and incapacity to struggle against temptation without his help and penitently confessed his sin of pride. By return of post came a letter from the starets, who wrote that Sergius's pride was the cause of all that had happened. The old man pointed out that his fits of anger were due to the fact that in refusing all clerical honors he humiliated himself not for the sake of God but for the sake of his pride. "There now, am I not a splendid man not to want anything?" That was why he could not tolerate the Abbot's action. "I have renounced everything for the glory of God, and here I am exhibited like a wild beast!" "Had you renounced vanity for God's sake you would have borne it. Worldly pride is not yet dead in you.

I have thought about you, Sergius my son, and prayed also, and this is what God has suggested to me. At the Tambov hermitage the anchorite Hilary, a man of saintly life, has died. He had lived there eighteen years. The Tambov Abbot is asking whether there is not a brother who would take his place. And here comes your letter. Go to Father Paissy of the Tambov Monastery. I will write to him about you, and you must ask for Hilary's cell. Not that you can replace Hilary, but you need solitude to quell your pride. May God bless you!"

Sergius obeyed the starets, showed his letter to the Abbot, and having obtained his permission, gave up his cell, handed all his possessions over to the monastery, and set out for the Tambov hermitage.

There the Abbot, an excellent manager of merchant origin, received Sergius simply and quietly and placed him in Hilary's cell, at first assigning to him a lay brother but afterwards leaving him alone, at Sergius's own request. The cell was a dual cave, dug into the hillside, and in it Hilary had been buried. In the back part was Hilary's grave, while in the front was a niche for sleeping, with a straw mattress, a small table, and a shelf with icons and books. Outside the outer door, which fastened with a hook, was another shelf on which, once a day, a monk placed food from the monastery.

And so Sergius became a hermit.

Chapter III

*A*t Carnival time, in the sixth year of Sergius's life at the hermitage, a merry company of rich people, men and women from a neighboring town, made up a troika-party, after a meal of carnival-pancakes and wine. The company consisted of two lawyers, a wealthy landowner, an officer, and four ladies. One lady was the officer's wife, another the wife of the landowner, the third his sister — a young girl — and the fourth a divorcee, beautiful, rich, and eccentric, who amazed and shocked the town by her escapades.

The weather was excellent and the snow-covered road smooth as a floor. They drove some seven miles out of town, and then stopped and consulted as to whether they should turn back or drive farther.

"But where does this road lead to?" asked Makovkina, the beautiful divorcee.

"To Tambov, eight miles from here," replied one of the lawyers, who was having a flirtation with her.

"And then where?"

"Then on to L————, past the Monastery."

"Where that Father Sergius lives?"

"Yes."

"Kasatsky, the handsome hermit?"

"Yes."

"Mesdames et messieurs, let us drive on and see Kasatsky! We can stop at Tambov and have something to eat."

"But we shouldn't get home tonight!"

"Never mind, we will stay at Kasatsky's."

"Well, there is a very good hostelry at the Monastery. I stayed there when I was defending

Makhin."

"No, I shall spend the night at Kasat-sky's!"

"Impossible! Even your omnipotence could not accomplish that!"

"Impossible? Will you bet?"

"All right! If you spend the night with him, the stake shall be whatever you like."

"*A discretion!*"

"But on your side too!"

"Yes, of course. Let us drive on."

Vodka was handed to the drivers, and the party got out a box of pies, wine, and sweets for themselves. The ladies wrapped up in their white dog skins. The drivers disputed as to whose troika should go ahead, and the youngest, seating himself sideways with a dashing air, swung his long knout and shouted to the horses. The bells-bells tinkled and the sledge-runners squeaked over the snow.

The sledge swayed hardly at all. The shaft-horse, with his tightly bound tail under his decorated breech band, galloped smoothly and briskly; the smooth road seemed to run rapidly backwards, while the driver dashingly shook the reins. One of the lawyers and the officer sitting opposite talked nonsense to Makovkina's neighbor, but Makovkina herself sat motionless and in thought, tightly wrapped in her fur. "Always the same and always nasty! The same red shiny faces smelling of wine and cigars! The same talk, the same thoughts, and always about the same things! And they are all satisfied and confident that it should be so, and will go on living like that till they die. But I can't. It bores me. I want something that would upset it all and turn it upside down. Suppose it happened to us as to those people — at Saratov was it? — who kept on driving and froze to death. . . . What would our people do? How would they behave? Basely, for certain. Each for himself. And I too should act badly. But I at any rate have beauty. They all know it. And how about that monk? Is it possible that he has become indifferent to it? No! That is the one thing they all care for — like that cadet last autumn. What a fool he was!"

"Ivan Nikolaevich!" she said aloud.

"What are your commands?"

"How old is he?"

"Who?"

"Kasatsky."

"Over forty, I should think."

"And does he receive all visitors?"

"Yes, everybody, but not always."

"Cover up my feet. Not like that — how clumsy you are! No! More, more — like that! But you need not squeeze them!"

So they came to the forest where the cell was.

Makovkina got out of the sledge, and told them to drive on. They tried to dissuade her, but she grew irritable and ordered them to go on.

When the sledges had gone she went up the path in her white dog skin coat. The lawyer got out and stopped to watch her.

It was Father Sergius's sixth year as a recluse, and he was now forty-nine. His life in solitude was hard — not on account of the fasts and the prayers (they were no hardship to him) but on account of an inner conflict he had not at all anticipated. The sources of that conflict were two: doubts, and the lust of the flesh. And these two enemies always appeared together. It seemed to him that they were two foes, but in reality they were one and the same. As soon as doubt was gone so was the lustful desire. But thinking them to be two different fiends he fought them separately.

"O my God, my God!" thought he. "Why dost thou not grant me faith? There is lust, of course: even the saints had to fight that — Saint Anthony and others. But they had faith, while I have moments, hours, and days, when it is absent. Why does the whole world, with all its delights, exist if it is sinful and must be renounced? Why hast Thou created this temptation? Temptation? Is it not rather a temptation that I wish to abandon all the joys of earth and prepare something for myself there where perhaps there is nothing?" And he became horrified and filled with disgust at himself. "Vile creature! And it is you who wish to become a saint!" he upbraided himself, and he began to pray. But as soon as he started to pray he saw himself vividly as he had been at the Monastery, in a majestic post in biretta and mantle, and he shook his head. "No, that is not right. It is deception. I may deceive others, but not myself or God. I am not a majestic man, but a pitiable and ridiculous one!" And he threw back the folds of his cassock and smiled as he looked at his thin legs in their underclothing.

Then he dropped the folds of the cassock again and began reading the prayers, making the sign of the cross and prostrating himself. "Can it be that this couch will be my bier?" he read. And it seemed as if a devil whispered to him: "A solitary couch is itself a bier. Falsehood!" And in imagination he saw the shoulders of a widow with whom he had lived. He shook himself, and went on reading. Having read the precepts he took up the Gospels, opened the book, and happened on a passage he often repeated and knew by heart: "Lord, I believe. Help thou my unbelief!" — and he put away all the doubts that had arisen. As one replaces an object of insecure equilibrium, so he carefully replaced his belief on its shaky pedestal and carefully stepped back from it so as not to shake or upset it. The blinkers were adjusted again and he felt tranquilized, and repeating his childhood's prayer: "Lord, receive me, receive me!" he felt not merely at ease, but thrilled and joyful. He crossed himself and lay down on the bedding on his narrow bench, tucking his summer cassock under his head. He fell asleep at once, and in his light slumber he seemed to hear the tinkling of sledge bells. He did not know whether he was dreaming or awake, but a knock at the door aroused him. He sat up, distrusting his senses, but the knock was repeated. Yes, it was a knock close at hand, at his door, and with it the sound of a woman's voice.

"My God! Can it be true, as I have read in the Lives of the Saints, that the devil takes on the form of a woman? Yes — it is a woman's voice. And a tender, timid, pleasant voice. Phui!" And he spat to exorcise the devil. "No, it was only my imagination," he assured himself, and he went to the corner where his lectern stood, falling on his knees in the regular and habitual manner which of itself gave him consolation and satisfaction. He sank down, his hair hanging over his face, and pressed his head, already going bald in front, to the cold damp strip of drugget on the draughty floor. He read the psalm old Father Pimon had told him warded off temptation. He easily raised his light and emaciated body on his strong sinewy legs and tried to continue saying his prayers, but instead of doing so he involuntarily strained his hearing. He wished to hear more. All was quiet. From the corner of the roof regular drops continued to fall into the tub below. Outside was a mist and fog eating into the snow that lay on the ground. It was still, very still. And suddenly there was a rustling at the window and a voice — that same tender, timid voice, which could only belong to an attractive woman — said:

"Let me in, for Christ's sake!"

It seemed as though his blood had all rushed to his heart and settled there. He could hardly breathe. "Let God arise and let his enemies be scattered . . ."

"But I am not a devil!" It was obvious that the lips that uttered this were smiling. "I am not a devil, but only a sinful woman who has lost her way, not figuratively but literally!" She laughed. "I am frozen and beg for shelter."

He pressed his face to the window, but the little icon-lamp was reflected by it and shone on the whole pane. He put his hands to both sides of his face and peered between them. Fog, mist, a tree, and — just opposite him — she herself. Yes, there, a few inches from him, was the sweet, kindly frightened face of a woman in a cap and a coat of long white fur, leaning towards him. Their eyes met with instant recognition: not that they had ever known one another, they had never met before, but by the look they exchanged they — and he particularly — felt that they knew and understood one another. After that glance to imagine her to be a devil and not a simple, kindly, sweet, timid woman, was impossible.

"Who are you? Why have you come?" he asked.

"Do please open the door!" she replied, with capricious authority. "I am frozen. I tell you I have lost my way."

"But I am a monk — a hermit."

"Oh, do please open the door — or do you wish me to freeze under your window while you say your prayers?"

"But how have you . . ."

"I shan't eat you. For God's sake let me in! I am quite frozen."

She really did feel afraid, and said this in an almost tearful voice.

He stepped back from the window and looked at an icon of the Savior in His crown of thorns. "Lord, help me! Lord, help me!" he exclaimed, crossing himself and bowing low. Then he went to the door, and opening it into the tiny porch, felt for the hook that fastened the outer door and began to lift it. He heard steps outside. She was coming from the window to the door. "Ah!" she suddenly exclaimed, and he understood that she had stepped into the puddle that the dripping from the roof had formed at the threshold. His hands trembled, and he could not raise the hook of the tightly closed door.

"Oh, what are you doing? Let me in! I am all wet. I am frozen! You are thinking about saving your soul and are letting me freeze to death . . ."

He jerked the door towards him, raised the hook, and without considering what he was doing, pushed it open with such force that it struck her.

"Oh — *pardon!*" he suddenly exclaimed, reverting completely to his old manner with ladies.

She smiled on hearing that *pardon.* "He is not quite so terrible, after all," she thought. "It's all right. It is you who must pardon me," she said, stepping past him. "I should never have

ventured, but such an extraordinary circum-
stance . . ."

"If you please!" he uttered, and stood
aside to let her pass him. A strong smell of fine
scent, which he had long not encountered,
struck him. She went through the little porch
into the cell where he lived. He closed the outer
door without fastening the hook, and stepped
in after her.

"Lord Jesus Christ, Son of God, have
mercy on me a sinner! Lord, have mercy on me
a sinner!" he prayed unceasingly, not merely to
himself but involuntarily moving his lips. "If
you please!" he said to her again. She stood in
the middle of the room, moisture dripping
from her to the floor as she looked him over.
Her eyes were laughing.

"Forgive me for having disturbed your
solitude. But you see what a position I am in. It
all came about from our starting from town for
a sledge-drive, and my making a bet that I would
walk back by myself from the Vorobevka to the
town. But then I lost my way, and if I had not

happened to come upon your cell . . ." She began lying, but his face confused her so that she could not continue, but became silent. She had not expected him to be at all such as he was. He was not as handsome as she had imagined, but was nevertheless beautiful in her eyes: his greyish hair and beard, slightly curling, his fine, regular nose, and his eyes like glowing coal when he looked at her, made a strong impression on her.

He saw that she was lying.

"Yes . . . so," said he, looking at her and again lowering his eyes. "I will go in there, and this place is at your disposal."

And taking down the little lamp, he lit a candle, and bowing low to her went into the small cell beyond the partition, and she heard him begin to move something about there. "Probably he is barricading himself in from me!" she thought with a smile, and throwing off her white dog skin cloak she tried to take off her cap, which had become entangled in her hair and in the woven kerchief she was wearing under it. She had not got at all wet when standing under the window, and had said so only as a pretext to get him to let her in. But she really had stepped into the puddle at the door, and her left foot was wet up to the ankle and her overshoe full of water. She sat down on his bed — a bench only covered by a bit of carpet — and began to take off her boots. The little cell seemed to her charming. The narrow little room, some seven feet by nine, was as clean as glass. There was nothing in it but the bench on which she was sitting, the book-shelf above it, and a lectern in the corner. A sheepskin coat and a cassock hung on nails by the door. Above the lectern was the little lamp and an icon of Christ in His crown of thorns. The room smelt strangely of perspiration and of earth. It all pleased her — even that smell. Her wet feet, especially one of them, were uncomfortable, and she quickly began to take off her boots and stockings without ceasing to smile, pleased not so much at having achieved her object as because she perceived that she had abashed that charming, strange, striking, and attractive man. "He did not respond, but what of that?" she said to herself.

"Father Sergius! Father Sergius! Or how does one call you?"

"What do you want?" replied a quiet voice.

"Please forgive me for disturbing your solitude, but really I could not help it. I should simply have fallen ill. And I don't know that I shan't now. I am all wet and my feet are like ice."

"Pardon me," replied the quiet voice. "I cannot be of any assistance to you."

"I would not have disturbed you if I could have helped it. I am only here till day-break."

He did not reply and she heard him muttering something, probably his prayers.

"You will not be coming in here?" she asked, smiling. "For I must undress to dry myself."

He did not reply, but continued to read his prayers.

"Yes, that is a man!" thought she, getting her dripping boot off with difficulty. She tugged at it, but could not get it off. The absurdity of it struck her and she began to laugh almost inaudibly. But knowing that he would hear her laughter and would be moved by it just as she wished him to be, she laughed louder, and her laughter — gay, natural, and kindly — really acted on him just in the way she wished.

"Yes, I could love a man like that — such eyes and such a simple noble face, and passionate too despite all the prayers he mutters!" thought she. "You can't deceive a woman in these things. As soon as he put his face to the window and saw me, he understood and knew. The glimmer of it was in his eyes and remained there. He began to love me and desired me. Yes — desired!" said she, getting her overshoe and her boot off at last and starting to take off her stockings. To remove those long stockings fastened with elastic it was necessary to raise her skirts. She felt embarrassed and said:

"Don't come in!"

But there was no reply from the other side of the wall. The steady muttering continued and also a sound of moving.

"He is prostrating himself to the ground, no doubt," thought she. "But he won't bow himself out of it. He is thinking of me just as I am thinking of him. He is thinking of these feet of mine with the same feeling that I have!" And she pulled off her wet stockings and put her feet up on the bench, pressing them under her. She sat a while like that with her arms round her knees and looking pensively before her. "But it is a desert, here in this silence. No one would ever know. . . ."

She rose, took her stockings over to the stove, and hung them on the damper. It was a queer damper, and she turned it about, and then, stepping lightly on her bare feet, returned to the bench and sat down there again with her feet up.

There was complete silence on the other side of the partition. She looked at the tiny watch that hung round her neck. It was two o'clock. "Our party should return about three!" She had not more than an hour before her. "Well, am I to sit like this all alone? What nonsense! I don't want to. I will call him at once."

"Father Sergius, Father Sergius! Sergey Dmitrich! Prince Kasatsky!"

Beyond the partition all was silent.

"Listen! This is cruel. I would not call you if it were not necessary. I am ill. I don't know what is the matter with me!" she exclaimed in a tone of suffering. "Oh! Oh!" she groaned, falling back on the bench. And strange to say she really felt that her strength was failing, that she was becoming faint, that everything in her ached, and that she was shivering with fever.

"Listen! Help me! I don't know what is the matter with me. Oh! Oh!" She unfastened her dress, exposing her breast, and lifted her arms, bare to the elbow. "Oh! Oh!"

All this time he stood on the other side of the partition and prayed. Having finished all the evening prayers, he now stood motionless, his eyes looking at the end of his nose, and mentally repeated with all his soul: "Lord Jesus Christ, Son of God, have mercy upon me!"

But he had heard everything. He had heard how the silk rustled when she took off her dress, how she stepped with bare feet on the floor, and had heard how she rubbed her feet with her hand. He felt his own weakness, and that he might be lost at any moment. That was why he prayed unceasingly. He felt rather as the hero in the fairy-tale must have felt when he had to go on and on without looking round. So Sergius heard and felt that danger and destruction were there, hovering above and around him, and that he could only save himself by not looking in that direction for an instant. But suddenly the desire to look seized him. At the same instant she said:

"This is inhuman. I may die. . . ."

"Yes, I will go to her, but like the Saint who laid one hand on the adulteress and thrust his other into the brazier. But there is no brazier here." He looked round. The lamp! He put his finger over the flame and frowned, preparing himself to suffer. And for a rather long time, as it seemed to him, there was no sensation, but suddenly — he had not yet decided whether it was painful enough — he writhed all over, jerked his hand away, and waved it in the air. "No, I can't stand that!"

"For God's sake come to me! I am dying! Oh!"

"Well — shall I perish? No, not so!"

"I will come to you directly," he said, and having opened his door, he went without looking at her through the cell into the porch where he used to chop wood. There he felt for the block and for an axe which leant against the wall.

"Immediately!" he said, and taking up the axe with his right hand he laid the forefinger of his left hand on the block, swung the axe, and struck with it below the second joint. The finger flew off more lightly than a stick of similar thickness, and bounding up, turned over on the edge of the block and then fell to the floor.

He heard it fall before he felt any pain,

but before he had time to be surprised he felt a burning pain and the warmth of flowing blood. He hastily wrapped the stump in the skirt of his cassock, and pressing it to his hip went back into the room, and standing in front of the woman, lowered his eyes and asked in a low voice: "What do you want?"

She looked at his pale face and his quivering left cheek, and suddenly felt ashamed. She jumped up, seized her fur cloak, and throwing it round her shoulders, wrapped herself up in it.

"I was in pain . . . I have caught cold . . . I . . . Father Sergius . . . I . . ."

He let his eyes, shining with a quiet light of joy, rest upon her, and said:

"Dear sister, why did you wish to ruin your immortal soul? Temptations must come into the world, but woe to him by whom temptation comes. Pray that God may forgive us!"

She listened and looked at him. Suddenly she heard the sound of something dripping. She looked down and saw that blood was flowing from his hand and down his cassock.

"What have you done to your hand?" She remembered the sound she had heard, and seizing the little lamp ran out into the porch. There on the floor she saw the bloody finger. She returned with her face paler than his and was about to speak to him, but he silently passed into the back cell and fastened the door.

"Forgive me!" she said. "How can I atone for my sin?"

"Go away."

"Let me tie up your hand."

"Go away from here."

She dressed hurriedly and silently, and when ready sat waiting in her furs. The sledge-bells were heard outside.

"Father Sergius, forgive me!"

"Go away. God will forgive."

"Father Sergius! I will change my life. Do not forsake me!"

"Go away."

"Forgive me — and give me your blessing!"

"In the name of the Father and of the Son and of the Holy Ghost!" — she heard his voice from behind the partition. "Go!"

She burst into sobs and left the cell. The lawyer came forward to meet her.

"Well, I see I have lost the bet. It can't be helped. Where will you sit?"

"It is all the same to me."

She took a seat in the sledge, and did not utter a word all the way home.

A year later she entered a convent as a novice, and lived a strict life under the direction of the hermit Arseny, who wrote letters to her at long intervals.

Chapter IV

*F*ather Sergius lived as a recluse for another seven years.

At first he accepted much of what people brought him — tea, sugar, white bread, milk, clothing, and fire-wood. But as time went on he led a more and more austere life, refusing everything superfluous, and finally he accepted nothing but rye-bread once a week. Everything else that was brought to him he gave to the poor who came to him. He spent his entire time in his cell, in prayer or in conversation with callers, who became more and more numerous as time went on. Only three times a year did he go out to church, and when necessary he went out to fetch water and wood.

The episode with Makovkina had occurred after five years of his hermit life. That occurrence soon became generally known — her nocturnal visit, the change she underwent, and her entry into a convent. From that time Father Sergius's fame increased. More and more visitors came to see him, other monks settled down near his cell, and a church was erected there and also a hostelry. His fame, as usual exaggerating his feats, spread ever more and more widely. People began to come to him from a distance, and began bringing invalids to him whom they declared he cured.

His first cure occurred in the eighth year of his life as a hermit. It was the healing of a fourteen-year-old boy, whose mother brought him to Father Sergius insisting that he should lay his hand on the child's head. It had never occurred to Father Sergius that he could cure the sick. He would have regarded such a thought as a great sin of pride; but the mother who

brought the boy implored him insistently, falling at his feet and saying: "Why do you, who
heal others, refuse to help my son?" She be-
sought him in Christ's name. When Father Sergius assured her that only God could heal the
sick, she replied that she only wanted him to lay
his hands on the boy and pray for him. Father
Sergius refused and returned to his cell. But next
day (it was in autumn and the nights were already cold) on going out for water he saw the
same mother with her son, a pale boy of fourteen, and was met by the same petition.

He remembered the parable of the unjust
judge, and though he had previously felt sure
that he ought to refuse, he now began to hesitate
and, having hesitated, took to prayer and prayed
until a decision formed itself in his soul. This
decision was, that he ought to accede to the
woman's request and that her faith might save
her son. As for himself, he would in this case be
but an insignificant instrument chosen by God.

And going out to the mother he did what
she asked — laid his hand on the boy's head and

prayed.

The mother left with her son, and a month later the boy recovered, and the fame of the holy healing power of the starets Sergius (as they now called him) spread throughout the whole district. After that, not a week passed without sick people coming, riding or on foot, to Father Sergius; and having acceded to one petition he could not refuse others, and he laid his hands on many and prayed. Many recovered, and his fame spread more and more.

So seven years passed in the Monastery and thirteen in his hermit's cell. He now had the appearance of an old man: his beard was long and grey, but his hair, though thin, was still black and curly.

Chapter V

*F*or some weeks Father Sergius had been living with one persistent thought: whether he was right in accepting the position in which he had not so much placed himself as been placed by the Archimandrite and the Abbot. That position had begun after the recovery of the fourteen-year-old boy. From that time, with each month, week, and day that passed, Sergius felt his own inner life wasting away and being replaced by external life. It was as if he had been turned inside out.

Sergius saw that he was a means of attracting visitors and contributions to the monastery, and that therefore the authorities arranged matters in such a way as to make as much use of him as possible. For instance, they rendered it impossible for him to do any manual work. He was supplied with everything he could want, and they only demanded of him that he should not refuse his blessing to those who came to seek it. For his convenience they appointed days when he would receive. They arranged a reception-room for men, and a place was railed in so that he should not be pushed over by the crowds of women visitors, and so that he could conveniently bless those who came.

They told him that people needed him, and that fulfilling Christ's law of love he could not refuse their demand to see him, and that to avoid them would be cruel. He could not but agree with this, but the more he gave himself up to such a life the more he felt that what was internal became external, and that the fount of living water within him dried up, and that what he did now was done more and more for men and less and less for God.

Whether he admonished people, or simply blessed them, or prayed for the sick, or advised people about their lives, or listened to expressions of gratitude from those he had helped by precepts, or alms, or healing (as they assured him) — he could not help being pleased at it, and could not be indifferent to the results of his activity and to the influence he exerted. He thought himself a shining light, and the more he felt this the more was he conscious of a weakening, a dying down of the divine light of truth that shone within him.

"In how far is what I do for God and in how far is it for men?" That was the question that insistently tormented him and to which he was not so much unable to give himself an answer as unable to face the answer.

In the depth of his soul he felt that the devil had substituted an activity for men in place of his former activity for God. He felt this because, just as it had formerly been hard for him to be torn from his solitude so now that

solitude itself was hard for him. He was oppressed and wearied by visitors, but at the bot-
tom of his heart he was glad of their presence
and glad of the praise they heaped upon him.

There was a time when he decided to go
away and hide. He even planned all that was
necessary for that purpose. He prepared for
himself a peasant's shirt, trousers, coat, and cap.
He explained that he wanted these to give to
those who asked. And he kept these clothes in
his cell, planning how he would put them on,
cut his hair short, and go away. First he would
go some three hundred versts by train, then he
would leave the train and walk from village to
village. He asked an old man who had been a
soldier how he tramped: what people gave him,
and what shelter they allowed him. The soldier
told him where people were most charitable,
and where they would take a wanderer in for the
night, and Father Sergius intended to avail himself of this information. He even put on those
clothes one night in his desire to go, but he
could not decide what was best — to remain or

to escape. At first he was in doubt, but afterwards this indecision passed. He submitted to custom and yielded to the devil, and only the peasant garb reminded him of the thought and feeling he had had.

Every day more and more people flocked to him and less and less time was left him for prayer and for renewing his spiritual strength. Sometimes in lucid moments he thought he was like a place where there had once been a spring. "There used to be a feeble spring of living water which flowed quietly from me and through me. That was true life, the time when she tempted me!" (He always thought with ecstasy of that night and of her who was now Mother Agnes.) She had tasted of that pure water, but since then there had not been time for it to collect before thirsty people came crowding in and pushing one another aside. And they had trampled everything down and nothing was left but mud.

So he thought in rare moments of lucidity, but his usual state of mind was one of weariness and a tender pity for himself because of that weariness.

It was in spring, on the eve of the mid-Pentecostal feast. Father Sergius was officiating at the Vigil Service in his hermitage church, where the congregation was as large as the little church could hold — about twenty people. They were all well-to-do proprietors or merchants. Father Sergius admitted anyone, but a selection was made by the monk in attendance and by an assistant who was sent to the hermitage every day from the monastery. A crowd of some eighty people — pilgrims and peasants, and especially peasant-women — stood outside waiting for Father Sergius to come out and bless them. Meanwhile he conducted the service, but at the point at which he went out to the tomb of his predecessor, he staggered and would have fallen had he not been caught by a merchant standing behind him and by the monk acting as deacon.

"What is the matter, Father Sergius? Dear man! O Lord!" exclaimed the women. "He is as white as a sheet!"

But Father Sergius recovered immediately, and though very pale, he waved the merchant and the deacon aside and continued to chant the service.

Father Seraphim, the deacon, the acolytes, and Sofya Ivanovna, a lady who always lived near the hermitage and tended Father Sergius, begged him to bring the service to an end.

"No, there's nothing the matter," said Father Sergius, slightly smiling from beneath his moustache and continuing the service. "Yes, that is the way the Saints behave!" thought he.

"A holy man — an angel of God!" he heard just then the voice of Sofya Ivanovna behind him, and also of the merchant who had supported him. He did not heed their entreaties, but went on with the service. Again crowding together they all made their way by the narrow passages back into the little church, and there, though abbreviating it slightly, Father Sergius completed vespers.

Immediately after the service Father Sergius, having pronounced the benediction on those present, went over to the bench under the elm tree at the entrance to the cave. He wished to rest and breathe the fresh air — he felt in need of it. But as soon as he left the church the crowd of people rushed to him soliciting his blessing, his advice, and his help. There were pilgrims who constantly tramped from one holy place to another and from one starets to another, and were always entranced by every shrine and every starets. Father Sergius knew this common, cold, conventional, and most irreligious type. There were pilgrims, for the most part discharged soldiers, unaccustomed to a settled life, poverty-stricken, and many of them drunken old men, who tramped from monastery to monastery merely to be fed. And there were rough peasants and peasant-women who had come with their selfish requirements, seeking cures or to have doubts about quite practical affairs solved for them: about marrying off a daughter, or hiring a shop, or buying a bit of land, or how to atone for having overlaid a child or having an illegitimate one.

All this was an old story and not in the least interesting to him. He knew he would hear nothing new from these folk, that they would arouse no religious emotion in him; but he liked to see the crowd to which his blessing and advice was necessary and precious, so while that crowd oppressed him it also pleased him. Father Seraphim began to drive them away, saying that Father Sergius was tired.

But Father Sergius, remembering the words of the Gospel: "Forbid them" (children) "not to come unto me," and feeling tenderly towards himself at this recollection, said they should be allowed to approach.

He rose, went to the railing beyond which the crowd had gathered, and began blessing them and answering their questions, but in a voice so weak that he was touched with pity for himself. Yet despite his wish to receive them all he could not do it. Things again grew dark before his eyes, and he staggered and grasped the railings. He felt a rush of blood to his head and first went pale and then suddenly flushed.

"I must leave the rest till tomorrow. I cannot do more today," and, pronouncing a general benediction, he returned to the bench. The merchant again supported him, and leading him by the arm helped him to be seated.

"Father!" came voices from the crowd. "Dear Father! Do not forsake us. Without you we are lost!"

The merchant, having seated Father Sergius on the bench under the elm, took on himself police duties and drove the people off very resolutely. It is true that he spoke in a low voice so that Father Sergius might not hear him, but his words were incisive and angry.

"Be off, be off! He has blessed you, and what more do you want? Get along with you, or I'll wring your necks! Move on there! Get along, you old woman with your dirty leg-bands! Go, go! Where are you shoving to? You've been told that it is finished. Tomorrow will be as God wills, but for today he has finished!"

"Father! Only let my eyes have a glimpse of his dear face!" said an old woman.

"I'll glimpse you! Where are you shoving to?"

Father Sergius noticed that the merchant seemed to be acting roughly, and in a feeble voice told the attendant that the people should not be driven away. He knew that they would be driven away all the same, and he much desired to be left alone and to rest, but he sent the attendant with that message to produce an impression.

"All right, all right! I am not driving them away. I am only remonstrating with them," replied the merchant. "You know they wouldn't hesitate to drive a man to death. They have no pity, they only consider themselves. . . . You've been told you cannot see him. Go away! Tomorrow!" And he got rid of them all.

He took all these pains because he liked order and liked to domineer and drive the people away, but chiefly because he wanted to have Father Sergius to himself. He was a widower with an only daughter who was an invalid and unmarried, and whom he had brought fourteen hundred versts to Father Sergius to be healed. For two years past he had been taking her to different places to be cured: first to the university clinic in the chief town of the province, but that did no good; then to a peasant in the province of Samara, where she got a little better; then to a doctor in Moscow to whom he paid much money, but this did no good at all. Now he had been told that Father Sergius wrought cures, and had brought her to him. So when all the people had been driven away he approached Father Sergius, and suddenly falling on his knees loudly exclaimed:

"Holy Father! Bless my afflicted offspring that she may be healed of her malady. I venture to prostrate myself at your holy feet."

And he placed one hand on the other, cup-wise. He said and did all this as if he were doing something clearly and firmly appointed by law and usage — as if one must and should ask for a daughter to be cured in just this way and no other. He did it with such conviction that it seemed even to Father Sergius that it should be said and done in just that way, but nevertheless he bade him rise and tell him what the trouble was. The merchant said that his daughter, a girl of twenty-two, had fallen ill two years ago, after her mother's sudden death. She had moaned (as he expressed it) and since then had not been herself. And now he had brought her fourteen hundred versts and she was waiting in the hostelry till Father Sergius should give orders to bring her. She did not go out during the day, being afraid of the light, and could only come after sunset.

"Is she very weak?" asked Father Sergius.

"No, she has no particular weakness. She is quite plump, and is only 'nerastenic' the doctors say. If you will only let me bring her this evening, Father Sergius, I'll fly like a spirit to fetch her. Holy Father! Revive a parent's heart, restore his line, save his afflicted daughter by your prayers!" And the merchant again threw himself on his knees and bending sideways, with his head resting on his clenched fists, remained stock still. Father Sergius again told him to get up, and thinking how heavy his activities were and how he went through with them patiently notwithstanding, he sighed heavily and after a few seconds of silence, said:

"Well, bring her this evening. I will pray for her, but now I am tired . . ." and he closed his eyes. "I will send for you."

The merchant went away, stepping on tiptoe, which only made his boots creak the louder, and Father Sergius remained alone.

His whole life was filled by Church services and by people who came to see him, but today had been a particularly difficult one. In the morning an important official had arrived and had had a long conversation with him; after that a lady had come with her son. This son was a skeptical young professor whom the mother, an ardent believer and devoted to Father Sergius, had brought that he might talk to him. The conversation had been very trying. The young man, evidently not wishing to have a controversy with a monk, had agreed with him in everything as with someone who was mentally inferior. Father Sergius saw that the young man did not believe but yet was satisfied, tranquil, and at ease, and the memory of that conversation now disquieted him.

"Have something to eat, Father," said the attendant.

"All right, bring me something."

The attendant went to a hut that had been arranged some ten paces from the cave, and Father Sergius remained alone.

The time was long past when he had lived alone doing everything for himself and eating only rye-bread, or rolls prepared for the Church. He had been advised long since that he had no right to neglect his health, and he was given wholesome, though Lenten, food. He ate sparingly, though much more than he had done, and often he ate with much pleasure, and not as formerly with aversion and a sense of guilt. So it was now. He had some gruel, drank a cup of tea, and ate half a white roll.

The attendant went away, and Father Sergius remained alone under the elm tree.

It was a wonderful May evening, when the birches, aspens, elms, wild cherries, and oaks, had just burst into foliage.

The bush of wild cherries behind the elm tree was in full bloom and had not yet begun to shed its blossoms, and the nightingales — one quite near at hand and two or three others in the bushes down by the river — burst into full song after some preliminary twitters. From the river came the far-off songs of peasants returning, no doubt, from their work. The sun was setting behind the forest, its last rays glowing through the leaves. All that side was brilliant green, the other side with the elm tree was dark. The cockchafers flew clumsily about, falling to the ground when they collided with anything.

After supper Father Sergius began to repeat a silent prayer: "O Lord Jesus Christ, Son of God, have mercy upon us!" and then he read a psalm, and suddenly in the middle of the psalm a sparrow flew out from the bush, alighted on the ground, and hopped towards him chirping as it came, but then it took fright at something and flew away. He said a prayer which referred to his abandonment of the world, and hastened to finish it in order to send for the merchant with the sick daughter. She interested him in that she presented a distraction, and because both she and her father considered him a saint whose prayers were efficacious. Outwardly he disavowed that idea, but in the depths of his soul he considered it to be true.

He was often amazed that this had happened, that he, Stepan Kasatsky, had come to be such an extraordinary saint and even a worker of miracles, but of the fact that he was such there could not be the least doubt. He could not fail to believe in the miracles he himself witnessed, beginning with the sick boy and ending with the old woman who had recovered her sight when he had prayed for her.

Strange as it might be, it was so. Accordingly the merchant's daughter interested him as a new individual who had faith in him, and also as a fresh opportunity to confirm his healing

powers and enhance his fame. "They bring people a thousand versts and write about it in the
papers. The Emperor knows of it, and they
know of it in Europe, in unbelieving Europe"
— thought he. And suddenly he felt ashamed
of his vanity and again began to pray. "Lord,
King of Heaven, Comforter, Soul of Truth!
Come and enter into me and cleanse me from
all sin and save and bless my soul. Cleanse me
from the sin of worldly vanity that troubles
me!" he repeated, and he remembered how often
he had prayed about this and how vain till now
his prayers had been in that respect. His prayers
worked miracles for others, but in his own case
God had not granted him liberation from this
petty passion.

He remembered his prayers at the com-
mencement of his life at the hermitage, when
he prayed for purity, humility, and love, and how
it seemed to him then that God heard his prayers. He had retained his purity and had
chopped off his finger. And he lifted the shriv-
eled stump of that finger to his lips and kissed

it. It seemed to him now that he had been humble then when he had always seemed loathsome to himself on account of his sinfulness; and when he remembered the tender feelings with which he had then met an old man who was bringing a drunken soldier to him to ask alms; and how he had received *her*, it seemed to him that he had then possessed love also. But now? And he asked himself whether he loved anyone, whether he loved Sofya Ivanovna, or Father Seraphim, whether he had any feeling of love for all who had come to him that day — for that learned young man with whom he had had that instructive discussion in which he was concerned only to show off his own intelligence and that he had not lagged behind the times in knowledge. He wanted and needed their love, but felt none towards them. He now had neither love nor humility nor purity.

He was pleased to know that the merchant's daughter was twenty-two, and he wondered whether she was good-looking. When he inquired whether she was weak, he really wanted to know if she had feminine charm.

"Can I have fallen so low?" he thought. "Lord, help me! Restore me, my Lord and God!" And he clasped his hands and began to pray.

The nightingales burst into song, a cockchafer knocked against him and crept up the back of his neck. He brushed it off. "But does He exist? What if I am knocking at a door fastened from outside? The bar is on the door for all to see. Nature — the nightingales and the cockchafers — is that bar. Perhaps the young man was right." And he began to pray aloud. He prayed for a long time till these thoughts vanished and he again felt calm and confident. He rang the bell and told the attendant to say that the merchant might bring his daughter to him now.

The merchant came, leading his daughter by the arm. He led her into the cell and immediately left her.

She was a very fair girl, plump and very short, with a pale, frightened, childish face and a much developed feminine figure. Father Sergius remained seated on the bench at the entrance and when she was passing and stopped beside him for his blessing he was aghast at himself for the way he looked at her figure. As she passed by him he was acutely conscious of her femininity, though he saw by her face that she was sensual and feeble-minded. He rose and went into the cell. She was sitting on a stool waiting for him, and when he entered she rose.

"I want to go back to Papa," she said.

"Don't be afraid," he replied. "What are you suffering from?"

"I am in pain all over," she said, and suddenly her face lit up with a smile.

"You will be well," said he. "Pray!"

"What is the use of praying? I have prayed and it does no good" — and she continued to smile. "I want you to pray for me and lay your hands on me. I saw you in a dream."

"How did you see me?"

"I saw you put your hands on my breast like that." She took his hand and pressed it to her breast. "Just here."

He yielded his right hand to her.

"What is your name?" he asked, trembling all over and feeling that he was overcome and that his desire had already passed beyond control.

"Marie. Why?"

She took his hand and kissed it, and then put her arm round his waist and pressed him to herself.

"What are you doing?" he said. "Marie, you are a devil!"

"Oh, perhaps. What does it matter?"

And embracing him she sat down with him on the bed.

At dawn he went out into the porch.

"Can this all have happened? Her father will come and she will tell him everything. She is a devil! What am I to do? Here is the axe with which I chopped off my finger." He snatched up the axe and moved back towards the cell.

The attendant came up.

"Do you want some wood chopped? Let

me have the axe."

Sergius yielded up the axe and entered the cell. She was lying there asleep. He looked at her with horror, and passed on beyond the partition, where he took down the peasant clothes and put them on. Then he seized a pair of scissors, cut off his long hair, and went out along the path down the hill to the river, where he had not been for more than three years.

A road ran beside the river and he went along it and walked till noon. Then he went into a field of rye and lay down there. Towards evening he approached a village, but without entering it went towards the cliff that overhung the river. There he again lay down to rest.

It was early morning, half an hour before sunrise. All was damp and gloomy and a cold early wind was blowing from the west. "Yes, I must end it all. There is no God. But how am I to end it? Throw myself into the river? I can swim and should not drown. Hang myself? Yes, just throw this sash over a branch." This seemed so feasible and so easy that he felt horrified. As usual at moments of despair he felt the need of prayer. But there was no one to pray to. There was no God. He lay down resting on his arm, and suddenly such a longing for sleep overcame him that he could no longer support his head on his hand, but stretched out his arm, laid his head upon it, and fell asleep. But that sleep lasted only for a moment. He woke up immediately and began not to dream but to remember.

He saw himself as a child in his mother's home in the country. A carriage drives up, and out of it steps Uncle Nicholas Sergeevich, with his long, spade-shaped, black beard, and with him Pashenka, a thin little girl with large mild eyes and a timid pathetic face. And into their company of boys Pashenka is brought and they have to play with her, but it is dull. She is silly, and it ends by their making fun of her and forcing her to show how she can swim. She lies down on the floor and shows them, and they all laugh and make a fool of her. She sees this and blushes red in patches and becomes more pitiable than before, so pitiable that he feels ashamed and can never forget that crooked, kindly, submissive smile. And Sergius remembered having seen her since then. Long after, just before he became a monk, she had married a landowner who squandered all her fortune and was in the habit of beating her. She had had two children, a son and a daughter, but the son had died while still young. And Sergius remembered having seen her very wretched. Then again he had seen her in the monastery when she was a widow. She had been still the same, not exactly stupid, but insipid, insignificant, and pitiable. She had come with her daughter and her daughter's fiancé. They were already poor at that time and later on he had heard that she was living in a small provincial town and was very poor.

"Why am I thinking about her?" he asked himself, but he could not cease doing so. "Where is she? How is she getting on? Is she still as unhappy as she was then when she had to show us how to swim on the floor? But why should I think about her? What am I doing? I must put an end to myself."

And again he felt afraid, and again, to escape from that thought, he went on thinking about Pashenka.

So he lay for a long time, thinking now of his unavoidable end and now of Pashenka. She presented herself to him as a means of salvation. At last he fell asleep, and in his sleep he saw an angel who came to him and said: "Go to Pashenka and learn from her what you have to do, what your sin is, and wherein lies your salvation."

He awoke, and having decided that this was a vision sent by God, he felt glad, and resolved to do what had been told him in the vision. He knew the town where she lived. It was some three hundred versts (two hundred miles) away, and he set out to walk there.

Chapter VI

*P*ashenka had already long ceased to be
Pashenka and had become old, withered, wrin-
kled Praskovya Mikhaylovna, mother-in-law of
that failure, the drunken official Mavrikyev. She
was living in the country town where he had had
his last appointment, and there she was sup-
porting the family: her daughter, her ailing neu-
rasthenic son-in-law, and her five grandchildren. She did this by giving music lessons to
tradesmen's daughters, giving four and sometimes five lessons a day of an hour each, and
earning in this way some sixty rubles (6 pounds)
a month. So they lived for the present, in expec-

tation of another appointment. She had sent letters to all her relations and acquaintances asking them to obtain a post for her son-in-law, and among the rest she had written to Sergius, but that letter had not reached him.

It was a Saturday, and Praskovya Mikhaylovna was herself mixing dough for currant bread such as the serf-cook on her father's estate used to make so well. She wished to give her grandchildren a treat on the Sunday.

Masha, her daughter, was nursing her youngest child, the eldest boy and girl were at school, and her son-in-law was asleep, not having slept during the night. Praskovya Mikhaylovna had remained awake too for a great part of the night, trying to soften her daughter's anger against her husband.

She saw that it was impossible for her son-in-law, a weak creature, to be other than he was, and realized that his wife's reproaches could do no good — so she used all her efforts to soften those reproaches and to avoid recrimination and anger. Unkindly relations between people caused her actual physical suffering. It was so clear to her that bitter feelings do not make anything better, but only make everything worse. She did not in fact think about this: she simply suffered at the sight of anger as she would from a bad smell, a harsh noise, or from blows on her body.

She had — with a feeling of self-satisfaction — just taught Lukerya how to mix the dough, when her six-year-old grandson Misha, wearing an apron and with darned stockings on his crooked little legs, ran into the kitchen with a frightened face.

"Grandma, a dreadful old man wants to see you."

Lukerya looked out at the door.

"There is a pilgrim of some kind, a man . . ."

Praskovya Mikhaylovna rubbed her thin elbows against one another, wiped her hands on her apron and went upstairs to get a five-kopek piece [about a penny] out of her purse for him, but remembering that she had nothing less than a ten-kopek piece she decided to give him some bread instead. She returned to the cupboard, but suddenly blushed at the thought of having grudged the ten-kopek piece, and telling Lukerya to cut a slice of bread, went upstairs again to fetch it. "It serves you right," she said to herself. "You must now give twice over."

She gave both the bread and the money to the pilgrim, and when doing so — far from being proud of her generosity — she excused herself for giving so little. The man had such an imposing appearance.

Though he had tramped two hundred versts as a beggar, though he was tattered and had grown thin and weather-beaten, though he had cropped his long hair and was wearing a peasant's cap and boots, and though he bowed very humbly, Sergius still had the impressive appearance that made him so attractive. But Praskovya Mikhaylovna did not recognize him. She could hardly do so, not having seen him for almost twenty years.

"Don't think ill of me, Father. Perhaps

you want something to eat?"

He took the bread and the money, and Praskovya Mikhaylovna was surprised that he did not go, but stood looking at her.

"Pashenka, I have come to you! Take me in . . ."

His beautiful black eyes, shining with the tears that started in them, were fixed on her with imploring insistence. And under his greyish moustache his lips quivered piteously.

Praskovya Mikhaylovna pressed her hands to her withered breast, opened her mouth, and stood petrified, staring at the pilgrim with dilated eyes.

"It can't be! Stepa! Sergey! Father Sergius!"

"Yes, it is I," said Sergius in a low voice. "Only not Sergius, or Father Sergius, but a great sinner, Stepan Kasatsky — a great and lost sinner. Take me in and help me!"

"It's impossible! How have you so humbled yourself? But come in."

She reached out her hand, but he did not

take it and only followed her in.

But where was she to take him? The lodging was a small one. Formerly she had had a tiny room, almost a closet, for herself, but later she had given it up to her daughter, and Masha was now sitting there rocking the baby.

"Sit here for the present," she said to Sergius, pointing to a bench in the kitchen.

He sat down at once, and with an evidently accustomed movement slipped the straps of his wallet first off one shoulder and then off the other.

"My God, my God! How you have humbled yourself, Father! Such great fame, and now like this . . ."

Sergius did not reply, but only smiled meekly, placing his wallet under the bench on which he sat.

"Masha, do you know who this is?" — And in a whisper Praskovya Mikhaylovna told her daughter who he was, and together they then carried the bed and the cradle out of the tiny room and cleared it for Sergius.

Praskovya Mikhaylovna led him into it.

"Here you can rest. Don't take offence . . . but I must go out."

"Where to?"

"I have to go to a lesson. I am ashamed to tell you, but I teach music!"

"Music? But that is good. Only just one thing, Praskovya Mikhaylovna, I have come to you with a definite object. When can I have a talk with you?"

"I shall be very glad. Will this evening do?"

"Yes. But one thing more. Don't speak about me, or say who I am. I have revealed myself only to you. No one knows where I have gone to. It must be so."

"Oh, but I have told my daughter."

"Well, ask her not to mention it."

And Sergius took off his boots, lay down, and at once fell asleep after a sleepless night and a walk of nearly thirty miles.

When Praskovya Mikhaylovna returned, Sergius was sitting in the little room waiting for her. He did not come out for dinner, but had some soup and gruel which Lukerya brought him.

"How is it that you have come back earlier than you said?" asked Sergius. "Can I speak to you now?"

"How is it that I have the happiness to receive such a guest? I have missed one of my lessons. That can wait . . . I had always been planning to go to see you. I wrote to you, and now this good fortune has come."

"Pashenka, please listen to what I am going to tell you as to a confession made to God at my last hour. Pashenka, I am not a holy man, I am not even as good as a simple ordinary man; I am a loathsome, vile, and proud sinner who has gone astray, and who, if not worse than everyone else, is at least worse than most very bad people."

Pashenka looked at him at first with staring eyes. But she believed what he said, and when she had quite grasped it she touched his hand, smiling pityingly, and said:

"Perhaps you exaggerate, Stiva?"

"No, Pashenka. I am an adulterer, a murderer, a blasphemer, and a deceiver."

"My God! How is that?" exclaimed Praskovya Mikhaylovna.

"But I must go on living. And I, who thought I knew everything, who taught others how to live — I know nothing and ask you to teach me."

"What are you saying, Stiva? You are laughing at me. Why do you always make fun of me?"

"Well, if you think I am jesting you must have it as you please. But tell me all the same how you live, and how you have lived your life."

"I? I have lived a very nasty, horrible life, and now God is punishing me as I deserve. I live so wretchedly, so wretchedly . . ."

"How was it with your marriage? How did you live with your husband?"

"It was all bad. I married because I fell in love in the nastiest way. Papa did not approve. But I would not listen to anything and just got

married. Then instead of helping my husband
I tormented him by my jealousy, which I could
not restrain."

"I heard that he drank . . ."

"Yes, but I did not give him any peace. I
always reproached him, though you know it is
a disease! He could not refrain from it. I now
remember how I tried to prevent his having it,
and the frightful scenes we had!"

And she looked at Kasatsky with beautiful eyes, suffering from the remembrance.

Kasatsky remembered how he had been
told that Pashenka's husband used to beat her,
and now, looking at her thin withered neck with
prominent veins behind her ears, and her scanty
coil of hair, half grey half auburn, he seemed
to see just how it had occurred.

"Then I was left with two children and
no means at all."

"But you had an estate!"

"Oh, we sold that while Vasya was still
alive, and the money was all spent. We had to
live, and like all our young ladies I did not know

how to earn anything. I was particularly useless and helpless. So we spent all we had. I taught the children and improved my own education a little. And then Mitya fell ill when he was already in the fourth form, and God took him. Masha fell in love with Vanya, my son-in-law. And — well, he is well-meaning but unfortunate. He is ill."

"Mamma!" — her daughter's voice interrupted her — "Take Mitya! I can't be in two places at once."

Praskovya Mikhaylovna shuddered, but rose and went out of the room, stepping quickly in her patched shoes. She soon came back with a boy of two in her arms, who threw himself backwards and grabbed at her shawl with his little hands.

"Where was I? Oh yes, he had a good appointment here, and his chief was a kind man too. But Vanya could not go on, and had to give up his position."

"What is the matter with him?"

"Neurasthenia — it is a dreadful complaint. We consulted a doctor, who told us he ought to go away, but we had no means. . . . I always hope it will pass of itself. He has no particular pain, but . . ."

"Lukerya!" cried an angry and feeble voice. "She is always sent away when I want her. Mamma . . ."

"I'm coming!" Praskovya Mikhaylovna again interrupted herself. "He has not had his dinner yet. He can't eat with us."

She went out and arranged something, and came back wiping her thin dark hands.

"So that is how I live. I always complain and am always dissatisfied, but thank God the grandchildren are all nice and healthy, and we can still live. But why talk about me?"

"But what do you live on?"

"Well, I earn a little. How I used to dislike music, but how useful it is to me now!" Her small hand lay on the chest of drawers beside which she was sitting, and she drummed an exercise with her thin fingers.

"How much do you get for a lesson?"

"Sometimes a ruble, sometimes fifty kopeks, or sometimes thirty. They are all so kind to me."

"And do your pupils get on well?" asked Kasatsky with a slight smile.

Praskovya Mikhaylovna did not at first believe that he was asking seriously, and looked inquiringly into his eyes.

"Some of them do. One of them is a splendid girl — the butcher's daughter — such a good kind girl! If I were a clever woman I ought, of course, with the connections Papa had, to be able to get an appointment for my son-in-law. But as it is I have not been able to do anything, and have brought them all to this — as you see."

"Yes, yes," said Kasatsky, lowering his head. "And how is it, Pashenka — do you take part in Church life?"

"Oh, don't speak of it. I am so bad that way, and have neglected it so! I keep the fasts with the children and sometimes go to church, and then again sometimes I don't go for months.

I only send the children."

"But why don't you go yourself?"

"To tell the truth" (she blushed) "I am ashamed, for my daughter's sake and the children's, to go there in tattered clothes, and I haven't anything else. Besides, I am just lazy."

"And do you pray at home?"

"I do. But what sort of prayer is it? Only mechanical. I know it should not be like that, but I lack real religious feeling. The only thing is that I know how bad I am . . ."

"Yes, yes, that's right!" said Kasatsky, as if approvingly.

"I'm coming! I'm coming!" she replied to a call from her son-in-law, and tidying her scanty plait she left the room.

But this time it was long before she returned. When she came back, Kasatsky was sitting in the same position, his elbows resting on his knees and his head bowed. But his wallet was strapped on his back.

When she came in, carrying a small tin lamp without a shade, he raised his fine weary eyes and sighed very deeply.

"I did not tell them who you are," she began timidly. "I only said that you are a pilgrim, a nobleman, and that I used to know you. Come into the dining room for tea."

"No . . ."

"Well then, I'll bring some to you here."

"No, I don't want anything. God bless you, Pashenka! I am going now. If you pity me, don't tell anyone that you have seen me. For the love of God don't tell anyone. Thank you. I would bow to your feet but I know it would make you feel awkward. Thank you, and forgive me for Christ's sake!"

"Give me your blessing."

"God bless you! Forgive me for Christ's sake!"

He rose, but she would not let him go until she had given him bread and butter and rusks. He took it all and went away.

It was dark, and before he had passed the second house he was lost to sight. She only knew he was there because the dog at the priest's house was barking.

"So that is what my dream meant! Pashenka is what I ought to have been but failed to be. I lived for men on the pretext of living for God, while she lived for God imagining that she lives for men. Yes, one good deed — a cup of water given without thought of reward — is worth more than any benefit I imagined I was bestowing on people. But after all was there not some share of sincere desire to serve God?" he asked himself, and the answer was: "Yes, there was, but it was all soiled and overgrown by desire for human praise. Yes, there is no God for the man who lives, as I did, for human praise. I will now seek Him!"

And he walked from village to village as he had done on his way to Pashenka, meeting and parting from other pilgrims, men and women, and asking for bread and a night's rest in Christ's name. Occasionally some angry housewife scolded him, or a drunken peasant reviled him, but for the most part he was given food and drink and even something to take with him. His noble bearing disposed some people in his favor, while others on the contrary seemed pleased at the sight of a gentleman who had come to beggary.

But his gentleness prevailed with everyone.

Often, finding a copy of the Gospels in a hut he would read it aloud, and when they heard him the people were always touched and surprised, as at something new yet familiar.

When he succeeded in helping people, either by advice, or by his knowledge of reading and writing, or by settling some quarrel, he did not wait to see their gratitude but went away directly afterwards. And little by little God began to reveal Himself within him.

Once he was walking along with two old women and a soldier. They were stopped by a party consisting of a lady and gentleman in a gig and another lady and gentleman on horseback. The husband was on horseback with his daughter, while in the gig his wife was driving with a Frenchman, evidently a traveler.

The party stopped to let the Frenchman see the pilgrims who, in accord with a popular Russian superstition, tramped about from place to place instead of working.

They spoke French, thinking that the others would not understand them.

"Demandez-leur," said the Frenchman, *"s'ils sont bien sur de ce que leur pelerinage est agreable a Dieu."*

The question was asked, and one old woman replied:

"As God takes it. Our feet have reached the holy places, but our hearts may not have done so."

They asked the soldier. He said that he was alone in the world and had nowhere else to go.

They asked Kasatsky who he was.

"A servant of God."

"Qu'est-ce qu'il dit? Il ne repond pas."

"Il dit qu'il est un serviteur de Dieu. Cela doit etre un fils de preetre. Il a de la race. Avez-vous de la petite monnaie?"

The Frenchman found some small

change and gave twenty kopeks to each of the pilgrims.

"*Mais dites-leur que ce n'est pas pour les cierges que je leur donne, mais pour qu'ils se regalent de the. Chay, chay pour vous, mon vieux!*" he said with a smile. And he patted Kasatsky on the shoulder with his gloved hand.

"May Christ bless you," replied Kasatsky without replacing his cap and bowing his bald head.

He rejoiced particularly at this meeting, because he had disregarded the opinion of men and had done the simplest, easiest thing — humbly accepted twenty kopeks and given them to his comrade, a blind beggar. The less importance he attached to the opinion of men the more did he feel the presence of God within him.

For eight months Kasatsky tramped on in this manner, and in the ninth month he was arrested for not having a passport. This happened at a night-refuge in a provincial town where he had passed the night with some pilgrims. He was taken to the police station, and when asked who he was and where was his passport, he replied that he had no passport and that he was a servant of God. He was classed as a tramp, sentenced, and sent to live in Siberia.

In Siberia he has settled down as the hired man of a well-to-do peasant, in which capacity he works in the kitchen-garden, teaches children, and attends to the sick.